You are Amy. Your horse, Acorn, has been stolen by the evil Shadow Rider. When the Good Knight of the Golden Dragon and his warriors pass your father's inn on their way to the KEEP OF THE ANCIENT KING, you volunteer to lead them. Maybe you'll find your horse there.

You might be a kid, but you're brave! And you can outsmart any creatures you meet on the way . . . you hope!

An evil, pig-faced guard approaches you as you slip the magic ring onto your finger. You feel tingly all over. You look for your hand, but it isn't there! You're invisible!

Now, will you try to find your horse and escape?

Or will you help the Good Knight fight the evil soldiers in the castle courtyard?

The choice is yours!

Keep of the Ancient King

by Mike Carr

Illustrated by Michael Fishel
Cover art by Keith Parkinson

TSR, Inc.

For Katy

KEEP OF THE ANCIENT KING
© 1983 TSR, Inc.
All Rights Reserved.

This book is protected under the copyright laws of the United States of America. Any reproduction or other unauthorized use of the material or artwork contained herein is prohibited without the express written permission of TSR, Inc.

Distributed to the book trade in the United States by Random House, Inc. and in Canada by Random House of Canada, Ltd.
Distributed in the United Kingdom by TSR (UK), Ltd.
Distributed to the toy and hobby trade by regional distributors.

DUNGEONS & DRAGONS, D&D, FANTASY FOREST, and PICK A PATH TO ADVENTURE are trademarks owned by TSR, Inc.

First Printing: October, 1983
Printed in the United States of America.
Library of Congress Catalog Card Number: 83-50984
ISBN: 0-88038-062-4

9 8 7 6 5 4 3 2

All characters in this book are fictitious. Any resemblance to actual persons, living or dead, is purely coincidental.

TSR, Inc.
P.O. Box 756
Lake Geneva, WI 53147

TSR (UK), Ltd.
The Mill, Rathmore Road
Cambridge CB1 4AD
United Kingdom

Stop!

Don't turn this page yet!

You're about to set out on not one, but many great adventures! Here's all you have to do—

To start your adventure, turn to page seven and begin. Read until you come to a set of choices. Pick one and follow the directions.

As you read, keep making choices and following the directions until the story ends. Then start at the beginning again and pick other choices. Each one will take you on a different adventure.

All right, go ahead and turn the page . . .

"Stay in sight of the inn, Amy. These days, you never know who might come down the road!"

"Don't worry, Father. I'll be careful!" As you close the door of the inn behind you, the sun bathes you in warmth. It feels good to be outside.

Climbing the hill behind the inn, you think about your father. You wish he could be happy again, instead of fearful. Life was a lot better for everyone before Nightshade, the evil skeleton wizard, and his soldiers came into the valley.

As you near the top of the hill, you hear hoofbeats. At the top, you see a group of riders coming across the meadow toward you. They're dressed in armor, and they carry swords and shields!

Just as you're about to run home in fear, you notice the sign of the Golden Dragon on their shields. They must be soldiers of the famous Good Knight!

Leading the group is a man on a big brown horse. "Hello!" he calls out.

"Good day!" you say excitedly.

"My name is Gregor," he says.

"You're the Good Knight!" you say. "I've heard many stories about you!"

Gregor nods. "These are my warriors. We want to bring peace to the land. We're headed to the Keep of the Ancient King, on a quest against the evil of Nightshade."

"I know where that castle is!" you tell him. "It's near here. Before Nightshade came and the king and queen fled, I used to play in the tunnels below the castle."

As you talk, you study the Good Knight's horse. What a beautiful animal he is!

The Good Knight sees you looking at his mount. "I can tell you like horses," he says. "My charger's name is Rex."

"I used to have a horse just like him," you say sadly. "His name was Acorn."

"What happened to him?"

"When Nightshade's evil soldiers came to my father's inn, they took whatever they wanted," you tell him. "A man wearing a dark, hooded cloak and called the Shadow Rider took my horse away.

"My father begged him not to take Acorn, but the Shadow Rider just laughed at him.

I cried, but the more I cried, the more he laughed. He's a terrible man!"

"Indeed he is!" agrees the Good Knight. "He brings death and sadness everywhere, carrying out Nightshade's orders. You're lucky to be alive, young one!"

"That's what the Shadow Rider said," you say. "He said many frightening things and made my father promise never to stand in Nightshade's way."

"And what about you?"

"I didn't promise anything. But I've been scared and lonely for a long time. Acorn was my only friend, the best horse anyone could want! And now he's gone, too."

"If we find him, we'll bring him back to you, little girl," the Good Knight promises.

"Please call me Amy. I'll do anything I can to help you!"

"Did you say there were tunnels below the castle?" Gregor asks.

"Yes, secret passages! But you'll never find them if you don't know where to look."

"If you know the way, you can help us, Amy," the Good Knight says.

"I could do something else to help you. Our family has a magic ring of invisibility hidden at home," you explain.

"Maybe that could get us into the castle instead of the tunnels," says the Good Knight. "Do you think you can get it?"

"Well, I'm not sure," you tell him. "My father might not like it after the warning the Shadow Rider gave him."

When you think of what the Shadow

Rider said, you feel a little scared yourself. Maybe you shouldn't help the Good Knight!

If you don't want to help the Good Knight, continue on to page 15.

If you want to run home and get the magic ring, turn to page 16.

If you want to show the Good Knight the secret tunnels, turn to page 18.

You really want your horse back, but your fear of the Shadow Rider is very strong. You think going to the castle would be too dangerous!

"I'm sorry, sir," you tell the Good Knight. "I think I'd better stay at home."

The Good Knight is surprised, but he understands. "That's all right, Amy. Can you just tell us where to find the tunnels?"

"Go over the next hill and follow the stream at the bottom," you explain. "You'll find the opening to the tunnels near a big stump."

"Thank you, Amy!" the Good Knight says. "We'll be back this way again!" He and his warriors ride away.

You wait for Gregor to come back, but he never does. When you hear that he was taken prisoner in the battle at the castle, you cry. Maybe you could have helped him win.

But it's too late now to change things. It looks like Nightshade will rule forever.

THE END

"I'll get the magic ring and help you!" you tell the Good Knight. "Wait here!"

You turn and run down the hill. A ring that makes someone invisible will surely be helpful in the fight against evil!

The thought of getting Acorn back makes you happy. It's about time somebody taught that Shadow Rider a lesson!

You wonder if you should say anything to your father. Would he help the Good Knight? Would he let you use the ring your grandfather gave to the family? Or would he be upset that you even talked to Gregor?

You know how much he's changed since the Shadow Rider came. He never talks about fighting evil anymore. He just wants to stay out of trouble.

As you enter the inn, your father looks up. "Back so soon, Amy?"

If you want to ask your dad to help the Good Knight, turn to page 23.

If you want to get the ring without telling your dad, turn to page 24.

"I'll show you the secret passages!" you say. "They're not very far from here."

"Fine, Amy. Let's go." The Good Knight lifts you up onto his horse.

Following your directions, the warriors soon locate the opening to the tunnels surrounded by trees and bushes. "It's well hidden," the Good Knight says. "We couldn't have found it without your help."

"We used to hide inside and have a lot of fun," you explain. "Now everyone says the tunnels are full of evil creatures."

"Fear not, Amy. We're ready for them."

The men light torches as you all head
into the tunnels. One warrior stays outside
with the horses.

A dwarf named Harbold walks with you
as you lead the way. Gregor and the others
are right behind. "This way!" you say when
the tunnel branches into two paths.

The light is poor, but something shines
on the floor ahead of you. "It's a wind
chime," you tell Harbold as you pick it up.

The chime is a long, thin silver tube. It
gleams in the torchlight as you put it into
your pocket. You keep going.

"There's a room up ahead," you tell everyone. "We used to play in it."

The torches flicker when you reach the room. A cold breeze blows from somewhere. "We go through the room," you tell the others. "The passage continues ahead."

"There's another tunnel over here," the Good Knight says. He draws his sword, and it glows brightly. "My sword glows when evil is near," he explains to you. "There must be evil in this other passage."

"I've never seen that tunnel," you say. "I'm sure the castle is the other way."

"Let's destroy the evil that lurks in this new tunnel," says one warrior.

"I think we should keep heading toward the castle," Harbold tells the Good Knight.

The Good Knight turns to you. "Which way should we go, Amy?"

If you want to go down the new tunnel, turn to page 31.

If you want to keep on going to the castle, turn to page 28.

"The Good Knight's on the hill," you say. "He's going to attack Nightshade and his forces in the castle! We can help the Good Knight. Maybe I can get Acorn back!"

Instead of being glad, your father is angry. "Silly child!" he says. "The Good Knight is brave, but he's also foolish. Nightshade and his evil soldiers are much too strong to be defeated."

"But, Father," you protest, "Sir Gregor has a company of warriors with him! And we can use our magic ring to help him!"

"Nonsense, girl! We'll do nothing of the kind. Now, stay inside!"

You don't want to disobey your father, but you must help Gregor defeat Nightshade! Then your father will be happy again.

When your father isn't looking, you slip out the back door, race over the hill, and join the Good Knight and his company.

"I couldn't get the ring," you say, trying to catch your breath.

"That's all right," Gregor says.

Please turn to page 18.

"I, uh, just came back to get a drink of water," you tell your father. He looks a little puzzled but doesn't say anything.

You go to the water jug in the hall and take a drink. Then quietly you step up onto a stool and reach above a shelf cluttered with bottles and bowls. You slip your hand inside a certain jug and feel the ring!

You grab it and quietly jump down off the stool. "Good-bye, Father!" you shout, running back out the door and up the hill.

"I have the ring!" you tell the waiting

Good Knight. "Watch this!" When you put it on your finger, you become invisible!

You can see how surprised and excited everyone is. When you take off the ring, you appear again. "That will help us a lot, Amy!" the Good Knight says.

"It's a small ring," you say. "I'm the only one who can wear it."

"That gives me an idea!" Gregor says. "Let's go directly to the castle instead of the tunnels." He lifts you up onto his horse. It's just like riding Acorn!

It isn't very long before all of you are on a hill, looking up at the castle.

"What do you think, Gregor?" Harbold the dwarf asks.

"It looks well defended," says the Good Knight, "but my idea just might work!"

He turns to you. "First, you must become invisible. Then, you'll climb that tree next to the wall and get inside the castle. When we attack, you'll open the gate so we can get inside. Do you think you can do it?"

If you agree to climb over the wall while invisible, turn to page 36.

If you'd rather not try anything so dangerous, turn to page 41.

"Let's keep going to the castle," you say, thinking of your missing horse. "It's still a long way from here."

"You're right," the Good Knight says. "Our quest is to get to the castle and destroy the evil there."

With the Good Knight, you, and an elf named Quickarrow in the lead, the journey continues. "We're getting close to the castle," you tell them.

Suddenly, an ugly green monster rushes out of the darkness. "A troll!" the Good Knight shouts, drawing his sword. The blade glows brightly as he swings it at the creature.

"Attack!" Harbold yells. He pushes past you with his sword.

The troll bites and claws, fighting ferociously. It pulls Quickarrow's shield away from him, and the elf retreats.

Gregor and Harbold each grab a torch and rush toward the troll. Seeing the fire, the troll runs away down another corridor.

Now that the ugly troll is gone, your company moves on, until the sound of voices

ahead makes everyone stop and listen!

"Those are dwarves!" Harbold says.

He's right! In a minute, three dwarves come down the tunnel toward you. "Ho, there!" the leader shouts.

"Ho, yourself!" Harbold says. "What are you doing here?"

"We escaped from Nightshade's dungeon. We're seeking a way out of here!"

"Did you see the Shadow Rider with a brown horse named Acorn?" you ask.

"The Shadow Rider killed a horse that didn't obey him," one of them says. "It could have been that one."

Acorn dead? The thought is too much to take! You can't help bursting into tears!

"I think you should go back home, Amy," the Good Knight says. "These dwarves can help us find the castle."

If you agree that you should go back home, turn to page 44.

If you want to keep going with the Good Knight, turn to page 46.

"Let's see what's in that tunnel," you tell the Good Knight, curious to look at the new passageway.

"Be careful," Harbold says. He and the Good Knight go ahead, and you and the others follow them.

As you walk along, the new tunnel gets wider and the ceiling becomes higher. There are pieces of rock on the floor.

"I wonder if something's been through here before us," Harbold says.

Suddenly there's a roar—and it's different from any roar you've ever heard.

"There's your answer!" the Good Knight says. "It sounds like a minotaur! Get ready!" he shouts. Everybody draws their weapons.

"Stay back, Amy," Harbold says to you.

Ahead, the tunnel opens up into a room. Across the room is a huge, bull-like creature with black fur. Its green eyes and sharp white teeth glisten in the torchlight. It is a minotaur! It roars again, this time so loudly

that the sound hurts your ears!

"Attack!" the Good Knight yells. Harbold and the others swarm toward the angry monster.

Now the fight is on! The minotaur growls and roars as it swings a mighty silver ax through the air.

You watch the Good Knight and the others fighting the creature. It's hard to tell who's winning!

Suddenly, you hear a weaker roar coming from a different direction. You turn toward the sound—and see a young minotaur, just about as tall as you are!

It's growling as loud as it can, trying to scare you. Because of its small size, though, the young monster doesn't seem as harmful to you as the big one.

Then it comes straight toward you!

If you want to get help from Gregor and the others, turn to page 51.

If you want to be friendly to the young minotaur, turn to page 50.

"I can do it!" you say. "I was inside the castle many times before Nightshade took it over. I know where to go. I'm ready!"

"We'll give you time to get over the wall," the Good Knight says. "When you hear us attack, open the gate."

"Why do you send a girl on such a dangerous mission?" asks one of the elves.

"This girl is brave," Gregor replies. "And you're foolish if you think only a man could do this!" He turns to you. "Do your best, Amy, and be careful!"

"I will," you reply. As you slip the magic ring onto your finger, your body tingles and you become invisible. You can't even see yourself!

You walk toward the castle. Of course, the evil men and creatures guarding the castle walls don't see you. You head for the tree beside the wall.

Behind you, the Good Knight and his troops start down the hill. The evil warriors see them and begin shouting. They're ready for battle!

When you reach the tree, you start climbing as fast as you can. You can hear the Good Knight and his men getting close to the castle!

Just as you jump from the tree onto the castle wall, you hear the Good Knight shouting. "We are here to rid this place of evil! Attack, men!"

Quickly, you race along the wall. You dodge the evil warriors as they rush past. Your heart pounds as you head for the gate.

You run down a stairway. At the bottom of it are two warriors guarding the gate. Though the gate is closed, you can see the rope that holds it shut.

Since the guards can't see you, you grab the rope and unwind it. The gate swings open, and the Good Knight and his men rush through the opening.

Now that you're inside, if you want to find your horse, turn to page 63.

If you want to help the Good Knight fight the evil ones, turn to page 57.

"That sounds awfully dangerous!" you say. "Isn't there another way?"

"I think we should just attack the place!" Harbold says. "That way, Amy won't be in such danger."

"Very well," the Good Knight agrees. "Form up for the attack!"

Everyone gets ready. The swords shine in the sunlight. "Wait here, Amy," the Good Knight says. You get off his horse and watch as everyone rides to the castle.

In a few minutes, the attack begins. As you start to cheer for the Good Knight, someone suddenly grabs you from behind!

"Cheering for the Good Knight, eh? You're a foolish little girl!" It's the Shadow Rider who has hold of you! He wears an evil grin.

"The Good Knight doesn't have a chance! My riders will surprise him from behind. Come!" He pulls you around. His men are waiting in back of you—and so is Acorn!

"My horse! My horse!" you shout. Acorn sees you and rears up. He remembers you!

"Quiet, girl!" the Shadow Rider snarls.

Then he mounts Acorn and pulls you up in front of him onto the horse's back.

The Shadow Rider and his warriors race toward the castle. Acorn's hooves thunder as the horses gallop after the Good Knight.

"Evil will triumph!" the Shadow Rider yells. Suddenly, the battle is all around you. The Shadow Rider holds you with one hand and swings his sword with the other. Evil warriors swarm out of the castle.

In a few minutes, the Good Knight and his men are defeated. The Shadow Rider

starts to laugh, but all you can do is cry.

"Don't cry, girl!" he orders. "I've got something for you—a chance to be with your horse forever! In fact, you can be with lots of horses. All you have to do is pledge your allegiance to Nightshade!"

If you choose to do what the Shadow Rider says, turn to page 71.

If you refuse to do what the Shadow Rider says, turn to page 66.

You don't want to cry in front of the others, but you can't help it. The thought of never seeing Acorn again is more than you can bear.

"Come, Amy," Quickarrow says. "I'll give you a ride home." You nod as you try to stop your tears.

The journey home seems long and sad. Quickarrow lets you down off his horse just outside your father's inn. Your eyes are still moist and red when he says good-bye.

"Take heart, girl," he says. "We have all suffered great sadness because of evil. Everything dear to us is in danger. That is why we must pledge our lives to the cause of good. Be strong, Amy. We will triumph."

As he waves good-bye, you have a new feeling inside you. Somehow, you know the elf is right—the evil will pass away. The times of sadness will be over, and peace will return to your land.

After so much sadness, it's something great to look forward to!

THE END

Bravely you fight back tears. "No, sir," you tell the Good Knight. "I'd like to keep going with you. I'll be all right."

"Very well," the Good Knight says. He turns to the three dwarves. "Will you help us attack the Keep?"

"We sure will!" the leader says. "We've got a score to settle with that Shadow Rider!" The others nod in agreement.

"Give them weapons!" Harbold says.

Each dwarf is given a sword. "On to the castle!" one dwarf shouts.

The Good Knight leads as the company sets out. When the tunnel splits, you point out the right way to go. Before long, you see a giant iron door blocking the path.

"I'll open it," the Good Knight offers. He pulls on the door, but it doesn't budge. When the dwarves try to help him, they can't open it either. Soon everyone is talking, trying to figure out what to do.

"I think it's magically locked," Harbold says. "We may never get it open!"

You try to wait patiently, but you get restless. You pull the chime out of your

pocket. You tap it on the wall to hear what it sounds like. It rings clearly.

"What was that?" the Good Knight asks. As he speaks, the door shakes, then opens!

"Zounds!" Harbold exclaims. "Was that noise from your chime, Amy?"

"Yes," you answer, surprised.

"Amy's got a magical chime of opening!" Quickarrow says.

"Let's go!" the Good Knight says. "Our attack will be a surprise if we hurry!"

"Evil must die!" Harbold shouts, running through the doorway after Gregor. Everyone follows. You run behind them and up a stairway. You're in the Keep!

The attack is a surprise, but the evil warriors fight back. All around you, the battle rages, but all you can think of is Acorn. You wonder if he is still alive.

If you want to go look for your horse, turn to page 76.

If you want to wait for the battle to end, turn to page 72.

"Hi, there!" you say as the small minotaur comes toward you. He sure looks as if he'd make a great pet.

But the young monster has another idea in mind. He thinks YOU will be a delicious meal!

And you are!

THE END

Even though it doesn't look very scary, it's still a minotaur! "There's another one!" you call out to the Good Knight.

"I'll slay it!" Harbold shouts. He runs past you just as the young minotaur shows its giant teeth. It's a good thing you called for help! The small monster lets out a roar and goes after Harbold.

In a couple of minutes, the fight is over. Both minotaurs are dead, and all is quiet. "Let's be on our way," Gregor says.

Then you hear a sound, far away. It sounds like the rattle of chains. "Wait. I hear something," you say. Everyone stops to listen.

"I hear it, too!" the Good Knight says. "It's coming from farther down the tunnel!"

"Let's go!" Harbold says. He and Gregor start running toward the sound. You hurry after them, trying to keep up.

Ahead, you hear the Good Knight shout, "It's a boy!" When you catch up, you see that you've entered a dungeon room of the Keep. And chained to one of the walls is a boy just a little older than you are.

"Help me!" he cries, rattling the chains. That's what the sound was!

"Free him!" the Good Knight says. Harbold swings his sword and breaks the chains. They fall to the floor.

"Thank you!" the boy says. "I was the next meal for those minotaurs!"

"They're gone," the Good Knight says. "But who are you, and why are you here?"

"My name is Jon. I am the prince of this land. The minotaurs had captured me."

"Jon?" the Good Knight says. "But we thought you were dead!"

"I've been hiding in these tunnels ever since my father's castle was taken. The minotaurs found me and brought me here. Thank you for rescuing me!"

"You're lucky, Prince Jon. Amy heard the sound of your chains. She's the one you should thank!"

The prince comes toward you. His clothes are torn and dirty, but he wears a big smile. "I owe my life to you, Amy! Are you from my father's kingdom?"

"Yes, your highness. I live quite near

here. My father is the innkeeper down the road."

"Call me Jon," he says, "and please be my friend from now on." Then he adds, "My father will be very grateful to you, I'm sure. I'll see that you're rewarded for saving my life!"

Your eyes open wide in surprise. The king's generosity is known throughout the kingdom. The reward could be something really special!

The Good Knight's voice snaps you out of your daze. "We must get the prince to safety right away. Lead us out of here, Amy. We'll come back to destroy the Shadow Rider and his master, Nightshade, later."

As you lead everyone back to the horses, you have a lot to think about—not only about yourself and your missing horse, but also about the battle between good and evil.

You're a part of that battle now, and there is much to be done. You know there are many exciting adventures ahead of you!

THE END

The battle is going on all around you.
Still invisible, you dodge the fighting men.

"Free us, Good Knight!" someone shouts.
The voice comes from across the courtyard,
and you run in that direction.

"Over here, Good Knight! Over here!" The
shouts come from several dwarves who are
imprisoned behind a large barred door.

Quickly, you look around and see a key
hanging on a hook on a nearby wall. You
grab the key and turn to the barred door.

The dwarves are staring at the key,
which looks as if it's floating in the air.
"What's going on?" one of them whispers.

"It's all right," you say. "I've come to help you escape."

The dwarves jump in surprise. "Who said that?" shouts one of them.

"I did!" you answer, pulling the magic ring off your finger. The dwarves are startled when you suddenly become visible.

"It's a little girl!" exclaims one dwarf. "How did you get inside the castle?"

"I came with the Good Knight," you say as you unlock the prison door.

When the door creaks open, the dwarves rush out. "Thank you, little girl!" several of them call out. Then the dwarf in the lead shouts, "Death to evil!" and they all race off to help the Good Knight.

Before long, the evil warriors are defeated, and the battle is over. One of the dwarves brings the Good Knight over to you and says, "That's her! That's the girl who set us free!"

The Good Knight smiles at you and puts his arm around your shoulders. "This battle was won because of your bravery. The dwarves turned the tide against evil. We owe you a lot! Please accept this gift as a reward for your help."

From behind the warriors, Harbold leads a horse. It's Acorn! And around his neck hangs a golden chain with a big, red ruby!

As you run to your horse, everyone cheers. It feels good to be a hero, but it feels even better to have Acorn back again!

THE END

The battle is raging throughout the castle, but all you can think of is Acorn. Is he still alive? You head for the stable.

You're lucky! All the evil warriors are busy fighting, and no one is guarding the stable. You race inside to look for your horse.

"Acorn! Acorn!" you shout. "Are you here?"

There are many horses in the stable, but only one is brown and looks like yours. It IS Acorn!

"Acorn, it's me!" you say, running over to his stall.

Acorn's ears perk up, but he seems to be afraid. Has he forgotten you? What's the matter?

Then you remember. You're still invisible! No wonder he's scared!

Quickly, you slip off the ring. When you become visible, Acorn neighs loudly, just as he always does when he sees you! He does remember you!

"C'mon, boy!" you tell him. "We've got to get out of this evil place!" You open the gate of his stall to let him out.

You lead Acorn out of the stable. You look around, but no one is watching you.

There's a big stone nearby, and you use it to climb up onto Acorn's back. Acorn prances a little, eager to get going.

"Let's go, Acorn! Giddyup!" you cry, and he takes off like the wind.

"The girl!" someone shouts. "Get the girl!" It's the evil Shadow Rider, and he's pointing at you! One of his warriors shoots an arrow, but it whizzes past your head.

Everything is a blur as you ride toward

the gate. The fighting is fierce all around you. You feel your heart pounding as you hold on tightly to Acorn's mane.

The castle gate is still open, and Acorn gallops through. He's free at last!

You ride on toward home, happier than you've been in a long time. You and Acorn will never be separated again! You hope that the Good Knight and his warriors will be as successful as you have been!

THE END

"No, never!" you shout. "I hate your evil! All it does is hurt people!"

Your words make the Shadow Rider angry. He dismounts and roughly pulls you down off the horse.

"So you don't like it, eh? Well, we've got a place for you!" He turns to one of his evil warriors. "Take her to the dungeon with the big spiders! She can think about evil for a long time there!" With an evil laugh, the Shadow Rider climbs back on your horse.

A dungeon filled with spiders! Nothing

could be worse than that! You know you've
got to do something, fast!

The big, ugly warrior is coming toward
you. The Shadow Rider is getting ready to
ride away. You must do something now!

You reach into your pocket. The magic
ring is still there! If you become invisible,
maybe you can get away!

Just as the evil warrior reaches you, you
pull the ring from your pocket. "Acorn!"
you shout to your horse. "Throw off the evil
one!"

Your horse obeys you! With a neigh, he rears up, and the surprised Shadow Rider falls to the ground. Quickly, you slip the ring on your finger. Now you're invisible!

"What's going on here?" the Shadow Rider yells. "Where's the girl?" He starts to pick himself up off the ground. You have to escape before he realizes what you're doing.

"Here I come, Acorn!" you shout. Your horse's ears perk up when he hears your voice. He's ready!

The evil warriors look around, but they can't see you. You run past one of them, grab hold of Acorn's saddle, and pull yourself up onto his back.

"Giddyup, boy! Go!" you cry.

In a flash, you're on your way. It feels great to be riding your horse again! The Shadow Rider and his men chase you, but Acorn is faster than all their horses.

At last, you're safe! Acorn is yours again, too. Wait till your father hears about this! He'll really be surprised!

THE END

To be with Acorn again is what you want more than anything else! "Yes, yes! I'll do it!" you tell the Shadow Rider. "Just let me be with my horse!"

"We'll have many horses for you, my pretty one! But you do understand that you can never change your mind again?"

"Being with Acorn is all I ever want!"

"Very well!" he says. You both dismount, and he puts his hands on your head. A strange, cold feeling comes over you. It's not like anything you've ever felt before!

It isn't long before you discover that you've made a terrible mistake. The magic ring doesn't work for you anymore. You never feel happy. And even being with Acorn isn't much fun.

A life of evil is worse than you ever thought it would be. The Shadow Rider and his warriors treat you badly. No one will be your friend. Everywhere you look, people are suffering because of evil. How could you have been so foolish?

THE END

You hide behind a pillar and watch the battle. In front of you, Harbold fights two ugly, pig-faced orc guards. When a third one tries to sneak up on him, you shout, "Look out behind you!"

Harbold turns around in time to save himself. In another minute, he's beaten all of them. "You saved my life, Amy!" he says.

Soon the battle is over. Many evil creatures are dead, and the rest have fled from the castle. The Good Knight and his men are victorious!

The Good Knight calls everyone together. "Victory is ours!" he says. "The Keep of the Ancient King has fallen! The bravery of this little girl made it possible. We salute you, Amy!" Everyone cheers.

It's nice to be a hero, but something else is on your mind. "What about my horse, Good Knight? Is he still alive?"

"We haven't found him, Amy. But the Shadow Rider escaped on a brown horse."

A brown horse! Was it Acorn? Maybe you'll never know! You start to cry, but the Good Knight comforts you.

"Don't cry, Amy. We know how much you loved your horse. There's no other horse that could mean as much to you. But we do have something else for you."

Quickarrow leads a beautiful white creature with a single, spiral horn toward you. It's a unicorn!

"Let this be your steed forever, Amy!" the Good Knight says. "Its magic will keep you safe against evil."

It's almost too good to be true! You've lost your horse, but in his place, this magical animal will carry you across a land now free of evil!

THE END

You run into the courtyard. Everywhere a fierce battle rages. It looks like the Good Knight is winning!

Then, across the courtyard, you see something. A dark, shadowy figure in a gray cloak is sneaking out of the stable on a horse. It's the Shadow Rider, with Acorn!

"My horse!" you shout, looking around for help. "The Shadow Rider is escaping!"

"I see him, Amy!" Quickarrow says. He shoots an arrow just as the Shadow Rider hits Acorn with a whip.

"Be true!" Quickarrow shouts to the arrow as it flies across the courtyard. The shot is perfect! The wounded Shadow Rider falls off Acorn's back onto the ground.

In a short time, the castle is captured. "The Shadow Rider is dead, Nightshade has fled, and evil is gone from this place," the Good Knight says. "It is a great day for all of us!"

As Acorn nuzzles your face, you nod in agreement. It's a great day for you, too!

THE END

FANTASY FOREST™ Books

Is your dragon dragging?

Do you both need to go on an adventure?

Why not Pick a Path to Adventure™ with these
FANTASY FOREST™ Books?

#1 THE RING, THE SWORD, AND THE UNICORN
#2 RUINS OF RANGAR
#3 SHADOWCASTLE
#4 KEEP OF THE ANCIENT KING

From the producers of the DUNGEONS & DRAGONS® Game